I Want My Tooth

D0382694

Tony Ross

Andersen Press
London

The Little Princess had WONDERFUL teeth.

She counted them every morning.
Then she cleaned them . . .

. . . then she counted them again.
She had TWENTY.

Some of her friends had fewer than twenty teeth.
But THEY were not ROYAL.

Her little brother, who WAS royal,
had NO teeth at all.

"Haven't I got wonderful teeth?" said the Little Princess.
"In smart straight lines," said the General.
"Shipshape and Bristol fashion," said the Admiral.

"Haven't I got wonderful teeth?" said the Little Princess.
"ROYAL teeth!" said the King.

So every night, the Little Princess cleaned
the royal teeth again.

"Your wonderful teeth are because you eat all the
right things," said the Cook.

"You can count them if you like," said the Little Princess.
"One . . . two . . . three . . . four . . .

"HEY," said the Cook. "This one WOBBLES!"

"AAAAAGH!" screamed the Little Princess.
"One WOBBLES!"

"AAAAAGH!" screamed the Maid.
"One WOBBLES!"

The wobbly tooth wobbled MORE each day.

But the wobbly tooth didn't hurt, and soon the
Little Princess enjoyed wobbling it.

And she wobbled it and wobbled it, until the terrible day the wobbly tooth disappeared.

"I WANT MY TOOTH!"
cried the Little Princess.

"You can have mine," said the Dentist,
"until your new one comes along!"
"I want my tooth NOW!" said the Little Princess.

Everybody in the Palace searched for the missing tooth . . .

. . . but it was NOWHERE to be found.
"I WANT MY TOOTH!" cried the Little Princess.

"SHE WANTS HER TOOTH!" cried the Maid.

"It's all right," said the Little Princess.
"I've FOUND it . . .

. . . HE'S got it!"